The Man Who Lived in A Hat

*To Kimberly—
Don't get
stuck in
a hat!
Janice Levy*

JANICE LEVY

illustrated by DAVE BROWN

HR
· for the evolving human spirit ·

HAMPTON ROADS
PUBLISHING COMPANY, INC.

Cover design by Grace Pedalino
Illustrations by David Brown

For information write:

Hampton Roads Publishing Company, Inc.
1125 Stoney Ridge Road
Charlottesville, VA 22902

Or call: 804-296-2772
FAX: 804-296-5096
e-mail: hrpc@hrpub.com
Web site: www.hrpub.com

If you are unable to order this book from your local
bookseller, you may order directly from the publisher.
Call 1-800-766-8009, toll-free.

Library of Congress Catalog Card Number: 00-105254
ISBN 1-57174-211-5
10 9 8 7 6 5 4 3 2 1
Printed on acid-free paper in China

To Rick, with all my love

There once was a man who lived in a hat.

Don't ask.

Things happen.

"You call this a house?" complained the man. "I don't think so."

He chewed a pumpernickel bagel. An ant crawled by and grabbed a crumb.

"It's bad enough to live in a hat," said the man. "Ants I don't need." He reached for the bug spray.

"Not so fast," said the ant. "Let's do some business." She held out her card. "Call me Sadie."

The man scratched his head. He didn't know from talking ants.

"Crumbs for a wish," Ant Sadie said. "Trust me. It's a good deal."

"Hmmm . . ." the man thought, looking around the hat.

"I deserve better than this. Get me an apartment in the city.

With a toaster and a big screen TV.

And a rocking chair; I could sit a little."

"What about me?" Ant Sadie asked.

"Wait awhile," said the man. "I'm outta here."

Ant Sadie did the Antsy-pantsy. She rubbed
her antennae three times. Suddenly . . .

The man was in an apartment in the city!

He toasted a pumpernickel bagel.

He watched a wrestling match on TV.

His rocking chair squeaked.

"Am I good or what?" Ant Sadie asked.

But the man complained, "I deserve better than this.

Get me a house in the country.

With a microwave and a satellite dish.

And a hammock; I could swing a little."

"What about me?" Ant Sadie asked.

"Wait awhile," said the man. "I'm outta here."

Ant Sadie did the Antsy-pantsy. She rubbed her antennae three times. Suddenly . . .

The man was in a house in the country!

He melted Swiss cheese on a pumpernickel bagel.

He watched Sumo wrestling from Japan.

His hammock swayed.

"Am I good or what?" Ant Sadie asked.

But still the man complained, "I deserve better than this.

Get me a mansion on a mountain.

With a cook and an indoor wrestling ring.

And a hot tub; I could soak a little."

"What about me?" Ant Sadie asked.

"Wait awhile," said the man. "I'm outta here."

Ant Sadie did the Antsy-pantsy. She rubbed

her antennae three times. Suddenly . . .

The man was in a mansion on a mountain!

He ate a pumpernickel bagel with cream cheese from a silver platter.

He cheered a wrestling match from a ringside seat.

His hot tub steamed.

"Am I good or what?" Ant Sadie asked.

But still the man complained, "I deserve better than this.

Get me a palace on an island.

With my own bakery and wrestling team.

And a daily massage; I could relax a little."

"What about me?" Ant Sadie asked.

"Wait awhile," said the man. "I'm outta here."

Ant Sadie did the Antsy-pantsy. She rubbed
her antennae three times. Suddenly . . .

The man was in a palace on an island!

Pumpernickel pies and cakes and bagels filled the bakery shelves.

His wrestling team wore purple capes.

His back unkinked.

"Am I good or what?" Ant Sadie asked.

But still the man complained, "I deserve better than this.

Make me the Ruler of the Universe.

With magicians to zap my food.

Crown me the Wrestling Champion of the World.

And bring me a chair to be carried on, so my feet never touch the ground."

"Oy, such a headache," Ant Sadie said. "Is nothing good enough for you?"

The man snapped his fingers. "Get with the program, Sadie."

Ant Sadie sighed. She did the Antsy-pantsy.

She rubbed her antennae three times.

Suddenly . . .

The man was right back in the hat.

And there he lived for the rest of his life,

in a house as empty as his heart . . .

. . . except for Ant Sadie, her lawyer Rose,

Max the hairdresser, her butler Milton,

the twins Bertie and Gertie, her personal

trainer Arnold, and anyone from the old

neighborhood who came by for some

crumbs to eat.

Hampton Roads Publishing Company is dedicated to providing
quality children's books that stimulate the intellect,
teach valuable lessons, and allow our children's spirits to grow. We
have created our line of *Young Spirit Books* for the evolving human
spirit of our children. Give your children
Young Spirit Books—their key to a whole new world!

Hampton Roads Publishing Company
publishes books on a variety of subjects,
including metaphysics, health, integrative medicine,
visionary fiction, and other related topics.

For a copy of our latest catalog, call toll-free
(800) 766-8009, or send your name and address to:

Hampton Roads Publishing Company, Inc.
1125 Stoney Ridge Road
Charlottesville, VA 22902

e-mail: hrpc@hrpub.com
Website: www.hrpub.com